Paris in the Spring with Picasso

by Joan Yolleck

pictures by Marjorie Priceman

schwartz & wade books · new york

A Note About This Story

During a trip to the library, where I spent time reading about the writer Gertrude Stein and her fascinating friends, I couldn't help wondering: How did they spend their day as they looked forward to a soirée at Gertrude's? The story that follows is what I imagined. And though I made it up, all the characters are real, and I'd like to think everything *could* have happened, one day in spring at the beginning of the twentieth century, during a magical time in Paris.

My greatest thanks to Anne Schwartz
for taking Gertrude Stein to heart,
Jill Lanois for her artistry,
and Ron Lanois, who
lived it in full color. —J.Y.

For Leo —M.P.

Text copyright © 2010 by Joan Yolleck
Illustrations copyright © 2010 by Marjorie Priceman
All rights reserved. Published in the United States by Schwartz & Wade
Books, an imprint of Random House Children's Books, a division of Random
House, Inc., New York. • Schwartz & Wade Books and the colophon are trademarks
of Random House, Inc. • Visit us on the Web! www.randomhouse.com/kids • Educators and
librarians, for a variety of teaching tools, visit us at www.randomhouse.com/teachers

Library of Congress Cataloging-in-Publication Data
Yolleck, Joan. Paris in the spring with Picasso / Joan Yolleck ; illustrated by Marjorie Priceman.—1st ed.
p. cm. Summary: Describes how some of Paris's famous artists and writers, such as Pablo Picasso, Max Jacob,
and Guillaume Apollinaire, spend their day before preparing to attend a party at Gertrude Stein's apartment.
ISBN 978-0-375-83756-2 (trade)—ISBN 978-0-375-93756-9 (glb) 1. Paris (France)—History—1870–1940—
Juvenile fiction. 2. France—History—Third Republic, 1870–1940—Juvenile fiction. 3. Paris (France)—Intellectual
life—20th century—Juvenile fiction. [1. Paris (France)—History—1870–1940—Fiction. 2. France—History—Third
Republic, 1870–1940—Fiction. 3. Paris (France)—Intellectual life—20th century—Fiction.] I. Priceman, Marjorie, ill.
II. Title. PZ7.Y785Par 2009 [E]—dc22 2008005867

The text of this book is set in Fournier.
The illustrations are rendered in gouache and ink on hot-pressed watercolor paper.

Marjorie Priceman has rendered illustrations of two paintings by Pablo Picasso,
Two Nudes and *Gertrude Stein*, both painted in 1906.
Photograph credits: Gertrude Stein, c. 1908: Yale Collection of American Literature, Beinecke Rare Book
and Manuscript Library. • Pablo Picasso: "Picasso at Home," photographer unknown, copyright © 2009
by the Penrose Collection, England. All rights reserved. • Max Jacob at the piano, 1910: Réunion
des Musées Nationaux/Art Resource, New York. • Guillaume Apollinaire, 1914: BHVP/
Roger-Viollet • Alice B. Toklas: Janet Flanner and Solita Solano Papers, Manuscript Division,
Library of Congress, Washington, D.C.

Book design by Rachael Cole

MANUFACTURED IN CHINA
10 9 8 7 6 5 4 3 2 1
First Edition

On any day of the week, if you cross Paris's Luxembourg Garden going west, you will come to a cobbled street called rue de Fleurus.

Follow it to number 27 and you will arrive at the home of Gertrude Stein and her brother, Leo. When you knock on the door, Hélène, the housekeeper, will let you in.

"*Bonjour*, hello. *Comment ça va?* How are you today?"

Upon entering the tiny hall, you might adjust your hat in the big oval mirror. If you've brought an umbrella, just leave it in the stand. Hélène will take you into the salon, but don't expect her to stay. She has cooking to do.

Every Saturday, no matter what the season, Gertrude and Leo hold a soirée, an evening party. Friends come for dinner and then, at around nine o'clock, the house is opened to anyone who might like to visit.

Mais attendez, wait! We're getting ahead of ourselves. It's still early and Gertrude's friends are just beginning their day. How will they spend it? Shall we visit with them and see?

Guillaume Apollinaire steps down from the train, on his way home from an overnight stay with his mother. Strolling along the avenues lined with stalls, he thinks, *There is no place more beautiful than Paris.*

When he sees a crowd gathered, Apollinaire crosses the
street. In front of everyone, an acrobat is setting a big red
ball on the ground. The acrobat jumps lightly on top and
begins to spin the ball with his feet. As it twirls, he dances
to the music of a violin played nearby. Only when it starts
to rain does he leap off and run for cover. The acrobat
gives Apollinaire an idea for a poem, and pulling
on his straw hat, he hurries home.

In his apartment on rue Léonie, Apollinaire takes out pen and paper. He imagines the spinning acrobat and remembers the diamond mirrors of his costume flashing like lightning before a storm.

He can almost hear the rap of thunder, until he realizes it is someone knocking at his door.

It is Marie Laurencin.

"Come in, Coco," says Apollinaire, using his girlfriend's nickname.

Apollinaire realizes he won't have time to write down his poem and thinks instead, *I'll tell the story tonight at Gertrude's soirée.*

"You look . . . as pretty as a picture," says Apollinaire.

"Thank you," Coco replies. "I've brought some sketches."

Pardonnez-moi, excuse me. I must interrupt for just a moment to tell you that these sketches are of Apollinaire and their friends Pablo and Fernande. While the couple looks at them, let's visit with Max Jacob, who lives up the hill.

Max's apartment is in a tumbledown building he named the Bateau-lavoir, the Wash-boat, because it reminds him of the laundry boats where women do washing. His dearest friend, Pablo, lives upstairs.

Max came in very late last night and fell asleep with all his clothes on. When he wakes, he makes a cup of sweet coffee and adds water to a vase of flowers. As he remembers that tonight is Gertrude's soirée, his eyes twinkle and he hangs his silk cape on the door. Then he leans a silver-handled cane up against it. When he sets his top hat out on the crumpled bed, his dreams about his father's tailor shop come back to him. Sitting down at his writing table, he begins to write:

Women left their buggies outside the shop under chestnut trees.
Back then I was very little and only came up to their knees.

"Max, tell us about the newest fashions," they all would tease.
And I showed them my favorite color: "Zinzolin, if you please!"

Then Father fixed their dresses, and after he pulled out the last pin,
The ladies would say, "We'll be back next season wearing zinzolin!"

The hours fly by. Max barely hears the patter of rain and only looks up when Pablo's dog scratches at his door and then scampers upstairs.

Pardonnez-moi, but I am going to stop the story once again. I want to say I am very curious to meet this Pablo. Let's visit with him while Max is working.

Written in chalk on the door outside Pablo Picasso's studio are messages from friends—"Tote was here," "Manolo is at the café."

Inside, Pablo stands barefoot, thinking about the painting he worked on all through the night. He painted quickly, squeezing paint from tubes and dropping them to the ground. He didn't bother to light the oil lamp but painted holding a candle in one hand and a brush in the other.

Sweeping a lock of hair from his forehead, Pablo
studies his painting of two women. Then he mixes
brown with some black and begins to work.

His brilliant black eyes never leave the canvas.

The women grow bigger, as if they have gained weight, and squarer, so that they look very strong.

That's better, thinks Pablo of his painting, and he puts down his brush and goes into an alcove to change for the party. When he returns, wearing his favorite polka-dot shirt, he rereads the note his girlfriend has left.

Pablo, I am out walking Frika. She was barking and I didn't want her to wake you.
—Fernande

Fernande's real name is Amélie but she has changed it, like other models in the neighborhood. A few seconds before she enters the studio, Pablo smells her perfume.

"Frika and I were caught in the rain and went into the Lapin Agile," says Fernande. "Hardly anyone was in the restaurant, but Frédé was playing his guitar and we stayed until the rain stopped."

Pablo dries Fernande's hair as Frika jumps at his side, wanting to play. Rubbing Frika's fur, he says, "I think I'll bring you to the soirée tonight."

"Bonne idée!" answers Max, who appears at the door, closely followed by Apollinaire and Marie.

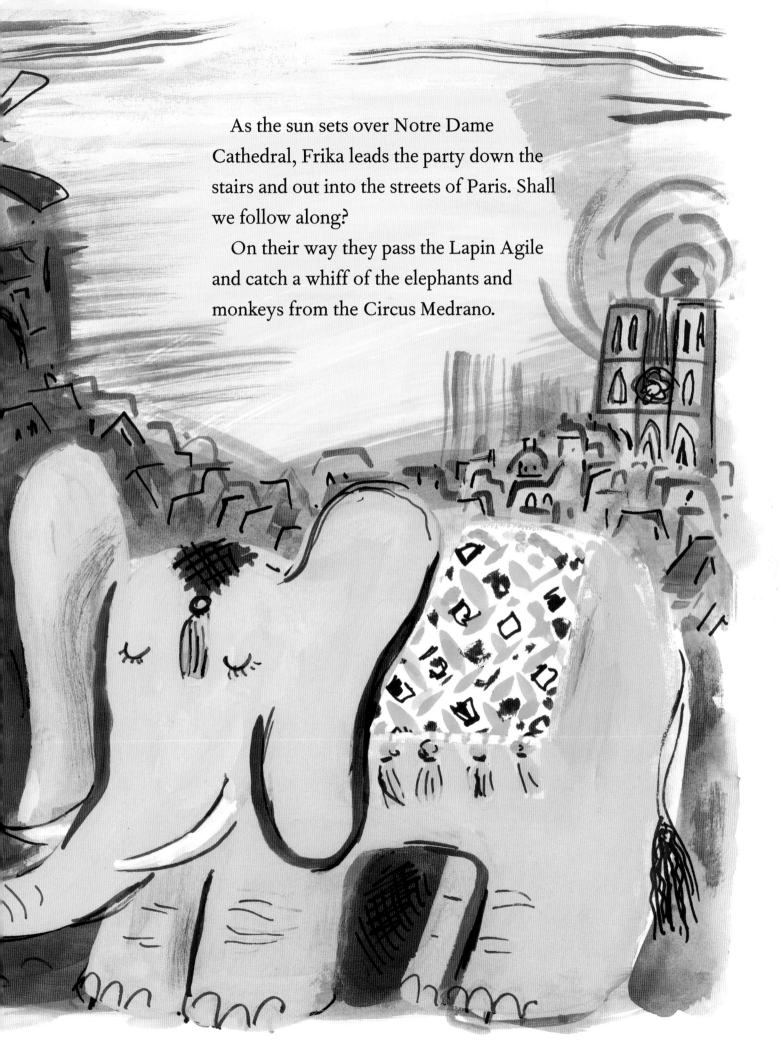

As the sun sets over Notre Dame Cathedral, Frika leads the party down the stairs and out into the streets of Paris. Shall we follow along?

On their way they pass the Lapin Agile and catch a whiff of the elephants and monkeys from the Circus Medrano.

They cross the river and glance into a cabaret, where a man in a red scarf and a black beret sings to the crowd. The electric streetlights go on. There are many things to do in Paris, yet they never stop on their way to Gertrude's salon. And you know, *mon ami,* neither would I.

Let's go ahead and visit with Gertrude before they arrive.

The salon is almost ready. Gertrude sits reading, in a big comfy chair, her feet tucked under her. Above the chair is a portrait of her painted by Pablo. In the picture she is wearing the same scarf and corduroy robe that she has on tonight.

Leo isn't home yet. He is in a café talking with friends. Hélène is busy in the kitchen.

As Alice B. Toklas, Gertrude's best friend, arranges cakes on the table, Gertrude hears her big Gypsy earrings jingle.

Looking up from her book, Gertrude says, "Sweetie, did you finish typing the pages I left for you this morning?"

"Yes, lovie," says Alice.

"And what did you think, my birdie?" asks Gertrude.

"I thought you must have been up late writing," says Alice. "It is very good."

Gertrude likes Alice's answer, and she chuckles as she gets up to fix the flowers. She smells one of the roses and whispers to herself.

"What are you saying, lovie?" asks Alice.

"I was saying," says Gertrude in her deep warm voice, "a rose is a rose is a rose is a rose."

"You are repeating," says Alice.

"I love repeating and you love my repeating," says Gertrude, chuckling again.

A knock at the door brings Hélène hurrying from the kitchen. *"Bonjour. Comment ça va?"* she says to Pablo and his friends.

Entering the hall, Fernande and Marie stop for a moment to adjust their hair in the big oval mirror. As Max tips his cane into the umbrella stand, he softly whispers, "Zinzolin would be the perfect color for an umbrella." Apollinaire tosses his straw hat onto the stand so that it catches and spins on the handle of Max's cane, like the acrobat twirling on his ball.

Pablo leads them into the salon and his
brilliant black eyes see Gertrude under
her picture, looking just as he painted her.
Hearing Frika bark a greeting, Gertrude lets
out a big, hearty laugh. Pablo laughs, too,
and the party begins.

As guests arrive, they look at the paintings
on the walls. They talk and laugh, and
between the tinkling of glasses I hear
the voices of our friends.

But it is getting late now, and it's time for bed. Tonight, under the stars that twinkle over Paris, I will dream of Gertrude's party. I wonder what everyone will talk about. *Que t'imagine,* my friend? What do you dream they will say?

More About the People You've Met in This Book

Gertrude Stein (1874–1946) was an American writer who lived in Paris with her brother, Leo, and later with Alice B. Toklas. She became friends with the artist Pablo Picasso after seeing his paintings in a gallery. A collector of works by experimental painters, including Picasso and Henri Matisse, she used Picasso's Cubist art style in her writing.

Pablo Picasso (1881–1973) is considered by many to be the greatest painter of the twentieth century. He was an artist who was constantly reinventing himself. Born in Spain, he lived his adult life in Paris in the company of a variety of women. Among his masterpieces are *Les Demoiselles d'Avignon, Guernica,* and his portrait of Gertrude Stein, which hangs in New York City's Metropolitan Museum of Art, as well as in Gertrude's salon in this book. Also in this book, Pablo is working on the painting *Two Nudes.*

Max Jacob (1876–1944) was a poet, painter, writer, and critic . . . as well as a generous and witty friend. Extremely poor, he shared a room with Picasso before they moved into their own apartments in the Bateau-lavoir, which you have visited in this story. Born Jewish, he converted to Catholicism and lived his later life in a monastery. He died in a Nazi concentration camp.

Guillaume Apollinaire (1880–1918) was born in Italy and grew up in France. A poet, playwright, and critic, he coined the term "surrealism." In 1911 he was accused of having stolen the Mona Lisa and arrested, but he was released from jail after five days.

Alice B. Toklas (1877–1967) was Gertrude Stein's lifelong companion. She came from San Francisco for a visit to Paris and stayed. Alice was a wonderful cook and the author of her own cookbook. She took care of household duties while Gertrude wrote books—one being a biography of Alice called *The Autobiography of Alice B. Toklas*.

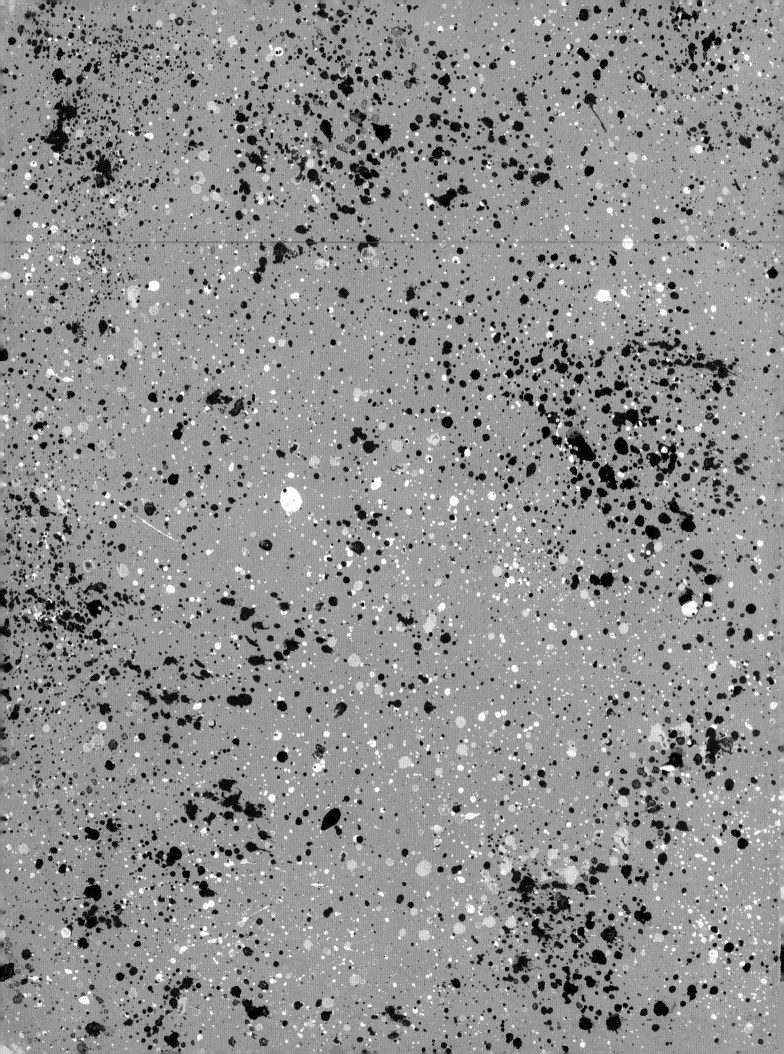